A SPEED BUMP & SLINGSHOT MISADVENTURE

NIGHT OF THE LIVING SHADOWS

Dave Coverly

SQUARE FISH

Christy Ottaviano Books

Henry Holt and Company New York

An imprint of Macmillan Publishing Group, LLC
175 Fifth Avenue, New York, NY 10010
mackids.com

Library of Congress Cataloging-in-Publication Data is available.
ISBN 978-1-250-12942-0 (paperback) ISBN 978-1-250-11341-2 (ebook)

Originally published in the United States by Christy
Ottaviano Books/Henry Holt and Company
First Square Fish edition, 2017
Book designed by Anna Booth
Square Fish logo designed by Filomena Tuosto

1 3 5 7 9 10 8 6 4 2

AR: 3.3 / LEXILE: 560L

For every librarian who's ever helped a kid
find a new favorite book,
and for every kid who's ever asked a librarian
for help finding a new favorite book

Don't miss these other books by Dave Coverly:

Night of the Living Worms: A Speed Bump and Slingshot Misadventure, Book 1

Night of the Living Zombie Bugs: A Speed Bump and Slingshot Misadventure, Book 2

Dogs Are People, Too: A Collection of Cartoons to Make Your Tail Wag

The Very Inappropriate Word, written by Jim Tobin

Sue MacDonald Had a Book, written by Jim Tobin

CONTENTS

HOLE,
SLEEPY
HOLE

ZERO

CHAPTER THAT SOARS

Speed Bump.

Speeed Buuump.

Hey.

Wake up.

Speedy.
Buddy.
Hey, hey, hey.
Wakey, wakey, eggs and bakey!

Hello?
Speedy?
Is this thing on?
Uh, Slingshot, that's not how it works.

Did you know you've been sleeping for 48 HOURS STRAIGHT?
Yeah, I DID know that. And I was really starting to enjoy hour number 49 before you woke me up.

After his daring adventure rescuing his brother, Early Bird, from the evil Nightcrawlers, Speed Bump had been so exhausted that he fell asleep while flying.

Luckily for him, he'd been right over a forest of soft Yellowwood trees and didn't even wake up when he landed. Slingshot put his buddy on his back and flew him all the way home.

Speed Bump hadn't even so much as twitched when Slingshot dropped him into his nest, stuck the headphones over his ears, and turned on Birdthoven's Symphony no. 7 in Beak-Flat Major.

But now that Speed Bump was awake, Slingshot had more important things on his mind.

"Aren't you STARVING? I can hardly go 48 MINUTES without eating!" Slingshot groaned.

"Not really. I still sort of have that nasty Nightcrawler taste in my mouth."

"Mmmm, Nightcrawlers . . . Well, I HAD to get you up. Today's the scavenger hunt, remember?"

Speed Bump and Slingshot were members of the Bird Scouts. It was their favorite club, and it was where the two of them had met when they were little, before their fuzzy baby feathers had even developed into flight feathers. They'd done all their activities together and earned all their Bird Badges except for one: the Scavenger Badge.

"Cheesable mercy, Slingshot! Is the scavenger hunt TODAY?"

"You bet! Why do you think I brought this stylish fanny pack?"

Slingshot put on his fanny pack while Speed Bump searched under his nest for his.

Check it out! I brought some of my treasures.
My lucky froggy foot.
This strange bent metal thing.
A cat's-eye marble!
Do you think it's a REAL cat's eye?

But I left room for all the stuff on our SCAVENGER HUNT list!
Hold still.

GOOD IDEA! What do we need to find again?
Wait, don't tell me.

SOMETHING THAT TURNS!
SOMETHING THAT BURNS!
SOMETHING THAT'S PINK!
SOMETHING THAT STINKS!

It's our last badge, Speedy! Our LAST BADGE! And then we'll be...

EAGLE SCOUTS!

Then Speed Bump and Slingshot ran around the room, wings out, pretending to soar and trying to shriek like eagles. Mostly they just sounded like squeaky toys, but they didn't care.

ONE

CHAPTER THAT'S NUTS

"Boy, I thought finding something that turns would be a lot easier than this," Slingshot said as the friends circled over a field.

They'd been flying for so long that Slingshot had already stopped twice to eat some roly-poly bugs and a few yellow berries that were extremely sour.

Yeah, my tail feathers are dragging, and my little wings are just about flapped out.
Hey, why don't we stop and ask those guys where we can find something that turns around here?

Dotted against the sky were rows of birds sitting on wires, all cheeping and chirping and chattering about nothing in particular. Bird gossip, mostly. Speed Bump and Slingshot squeezed in between a couple of raspy-voiced Blue Jays.

Wow, you don't skip many meals, do you?
How do you fly with such a big head?
Not judging, just genuinely curious.
Retweet!
Blue Jays were not known for their social skills.

"We're, uh, on a scavenger hunt," said Speed Bump.

"What's a scavenger? How do you hunt it?"

"Do you have weapons? Is your weapon in that funny little pouch around your big waist?"

No, it's just a game.
We're looking for something that turns.
Well, if you're LOOKING for something, you should talk to Nuthatch yammering down there. He collects stuff and never shuts up about it.

Excuse me, are you Nuthatch?

Yep, yep, yep! What's shakin'? Are you new here? You're new here, right? 'Cause I know EVERYONE on the wire and I don't know YOU! What're your names? I'm Nuthatch, yes sirree Bob but my friends just call me Nuts. You can call me Nuts, too. I'm sure we'll be good friends very, very soon!

Cheesable mercy, he talks FAST!
And who's Yes sirree Bob?
Okay, um, "Nuts." Well, I'm Speed Bump, this is Slingshot, and we're on a scavenger hunt.
That Jay told us you might be able to help.

Holy Crow, boys, I'm your bird! I'm a born explorer! A scavenger hunt? Why didn't you SAY so?
Wait, you DID say so! HA! C'mon, follow me. I know just the place!

They flew together, following the wire and passing telephone pole after telephone pole. Sometimes Nuts and Slingshot had to fly a little slower so Speed Bump could catch up.

By the way, we're also searching for something that's pink, something that burns, and...
Something that stinks!

"Not to worry, my new friends," Nuts replied as they swerved around a wind turbine. "The place I'm taking you to has

EVERYTHING."

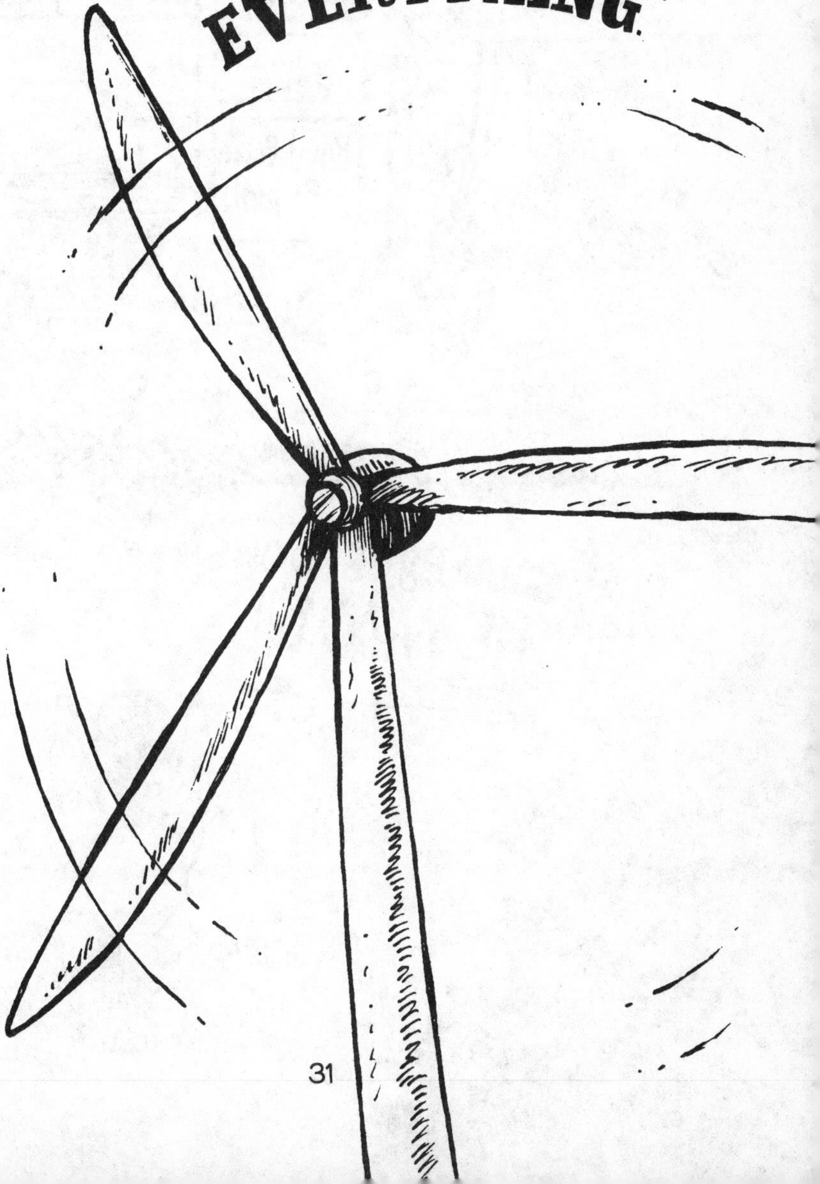

FOREST EDGE MALL
Abirdcrombie and Finch
Jay Crew
Chickadee Bauer
Bird Bath & Beyond
Feast your eyes, boys! It's THE MALL!

Tailbots
GRAND OPENING
Starbeaks
SKYWALK
PeckSun
heronpostale
Cheez.
A.
Bull.
MERCY!

"They call it the mall. I'm not sure what it's for, but I like it. People come here to collect things—they walk in with no bags and walk out with lots of them, and they're all full! I'm telling you, they've got EVERYTHING here. You'll find more scavenger hunt stuff than you can shake a tail feather at!"

"Whoa," the friends said. They tried to high-five each other, but it was more of a low five because Speed Bump's wing didn't reach above his head.

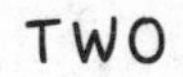

CHAPTER WITH STORES

"And the best part? There's food! Tons and tons of food! I mean, look at the people! Look how much they eat! Have you ever tried bread crumbs? You HAVE to try bread crumbs. Now, there's a meal that'll stick to your birdcage. But we'd better get in there fast. I think I just heard thunder!" Nuts looked up at the sky. It was cloudless.

"That was my stomach," Slingshot said proudly.

"Impressive. Okay, stay right behind me. I know a way to get inside."

"But it looks completely open!" Speed Bump said. "Why can't we just fly through the main entrance?"

FOOD
COURT
FOOD
MORE FOOD

"Oh, no no no no no," Nuts said. The feathers on his face quivered. "NEVER try to fly right in. It LOOKS open, but it's a trick. An evil trick! Those are called windows. Just because you can SEE through them doesn't mean you can GET through them. Believe me—I've made that mistake too many times!"

Speed Bump and Slingshot followed Nuts down to the front of the mall and landed on top of a trash can.

"This big window is really a door. Now we wait for people to open it so we can fly through. Not just one person, though—that doesn't give you enough time." Nuts shuddered at a memory. "When a bunch of people go in together, we go in with them, straight and fast, right over their heads."

Straight and fast? I CAN'T go straight and fast!
Don't worry, *mon ami*! Just grab my tail feathers with your beak and hold on tight!

A group of girls! Get ready!
Grab Slingshot's tail!
Now FLY!

As soon as they were inside, Speed Bump let go of Slingshot's tail feathers, and they flew to the top of a statue in the center of the mall.

Nuts gestured grandly with his wing.

"Take a gander around you, boys. More goodies than you could ever need!"

"This place is crazy!" said Speed Bump.

"Where do we even begin our scavenger hunt?" asked Slingshot.

"Good question, good question," said Nuts. "I see people looking at that board a lot. Maybe it will help."

They stared and stared at the directory.

"Nope."

"I got nothin'."

"Well, let's just start at the top of that moving stairs contraption."

That was FUN!
Why didn't you just FLY up?
Let's EXPLORE!

Owllister

WHOOOOOAAAA!

BUILD·A·BIR
Nice lederhosen!
Nice, um. Kilt?
OOPS.
Look what I found!
DOVE LOTION
Glam Glitter

THE PEACLOCK SHOPPE
I think that poor guy has lost his marbles.
CUCKOO! CUCKOO!
12
9
3
6

CAR SHOW
① "The Road Runner"

Say SELFIE!

BIRKENSTORR
MASSAGE CHAIR
TRY IT!

Pizza Parrot
I can't stop eating these pizza crust crumbs!
I know, right? Have you guys tried a french fry?
Pieces of cookie WITH CHOCOLATE STILL IN THEM!

Then they ate and ate and ate until they could barely fly to the ceiling rafters.

GROOOAAANN
I don't feel so good.
I sure didn't need that last cinnamon pretzel.
I should have warned you about the food! It's tasty but not so easy on the belly.

So... tired...
ZZZZZZZZZZ
Huh?
!
ATTENTION, SHOPPERS, THE FOREST EDGE MALL IS NOW CLOSED.

But they were too late.

THREE

CHAPTER WITH GUTS

I DON'T KNOW! This has never happened to me before!
Maybe there's another way out?

They flew down the corridors and checked every door. All of them were locked tight, and besides, the three birds weren't big enough to push them open anyway.

Suddenly, the mall didn't seem quite so fun. In fact, it seemed kind of scary.

This place is as creepy as a room full of Nightcrawlers! I HAVE TO GET OUT OF HERE!

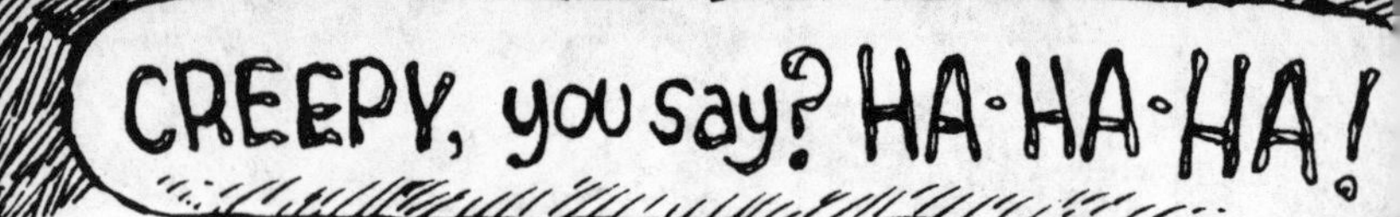

A grimy, disheveled bird with sticky-looking feathers popped up from the garbage can next to them. Speed Bump screamed and jumped into Slingshot's arms, and Nuts jumped onto his back.

It's not creepy—it's GLORIOUS! It's PARADISE! Why would anyone want to EVER leave the MALL? HA-HA-ha...ha...hack hack...
Whoa.
Pork rind?
Sorry, got a pork rind stuck in my throat.

"You outside birds don't know what you're MISSING! All these smells!" The bird held a half-eaten taco to his beak. "All these STORES! Look around! It's like this stuff is surrounding you and giving you a giant, squeezy hug and making you feel SAFE! Not like the outside, no sir!"

But we don't WANT to be here! We got trapped inside when the doors were locked!

"I got trapped, too!" the bird said. "I escaped, but then I got trapped again! And again! And then I started to LIKE it! I mean, REALLY like it! And now I'll NEVER leave! NEVER! HA-HA-HA-HA-HA-HA-HA!" His eyes rolled back in his head as he laughed, and each eye looked in a different direction before they focused back on Speed Bump. Then the scrappy old bird scooped up a wing full of garbage.

And before the three birds could say anything, he dove back into the can.

CAT PAUSE
What.
Was.
THAT?

THAT could be US if we stay in this place too long!
YIKES!
C'mon, let's hide out until morning and then get the heck OUT OF HERE!

The three of them flew to a nook in the rafters. Slingshot unzipped his fanny pack and pulled out three french fries.

"I really shouldn't, but . . ." said Nuts.

"How can you even think about eating when . . . yeah, okay, I'll take one," said Speed Bump.

A few minutes later, with bellies full and beaks greasy, they were fast asleep. Again.

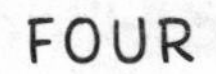

CHAPTER THAT'S GLASS

Sunlight streamed in through the mall skylight. Nuts ruffled his feathers and wiped his beak with a wing.

"It's open," he hollered. "Holy Crow, it's open! Let's GO!"

Speed Bump and Slingshot scrambled off the rafters and flew after Nuts as fast as they could, high above the morning shoppers and the smell of roasting coffee in the café. The birds spotted an older couple, wearing matching jogging suits, who were power walking straight toward the door outside.

THEM!
Speed Bump flapped his tiny wings as fast as he could, but it wasn't enough.
Slingshot, WAIT! Let me hold on to your tail!

But everything was happening too fast and Slingshot didn't hear his friend. He and Nuts zipped through the open door and up into the clear blue sky. Speed Bump was a second too late and flew headfirst into the glass.

Everything went blurry. He saw stars and worms around his head. Finally, Speed Bump came to his senses and realized he was sitting on the mall floor. His fanny pack had broken his fall.

Speed Bump began to panic. He didn't want to be alone. He didn't want to be stuck in the mall forever. And he DEFINITELY didn't want to live in a sticky garbage can and eat pork rinds every day.

He looked around for a place to hide. That was when he saw a lady heading for the exit. She had a big purse, and it was unzipped. Maybe it was his ticket outside! He hopped onto a short wall, pushed off, and aimed himself as straight as he could toward the opening.

HE MADE IT!

It was crowded inside the purse, and it smelled weird. Speed Bump was just about to pat himself on the back for his exit plan when he heard a horrible noise.

The lady was zipping her purse closed!

OH NO!
MY GOOSE IS COOKED!
ALBATROSS ASPIRIN
PUFFY PUFFIN TISSUES
OKABURRA
JayBan

Speed Bump was wedged between strange objects as he bounced around in the dark. A door slammed. An engine roared. Music started playing on the radio. Then they were on the move.

FIVE

CHAPTER WITH WINGS

Outside the mall, Slingshot and Nuts had been watching through the glass door when Speed Bump flew into the lady's purse. They kept an eye on her and hovered above as she walked to her car.

Bloominquails
APPLEBEAKS

F E
EXIT
SEE YOU
TOMORROW

Nuts started freaking out as the car drove away.

"Good plan, good plan!" said Nuts.

"I'd better, um, 'go'—*ahem*—you know!—on top of it so we don't forget which one it is."

"Now, that's using your head! Well, maybe not your head, exactly, but you know what I mean. . . ."

Slingshot cleared his throat.

After Slingshot was done marking the car, he and Nuts followed along, staying low so they wouldn't lose sight of it. The pair shot around stoplights, skimmed over street signs, and ducked under bridges as the lady drove toward the edge of the city.

"Uh-oh!" Nuts suddenly shouted over the traffic noise. "She's heading for the highway! We'll never keep up!"

Slingshot lowered his head, lifted his tail feathers, and zoomed down next to the car.

"I can see the purse in the backseat! And the window's open! Just a little bit, but I think I can squeeze through!"

"No, it's too dangerous! She's driving really fast. You'll never time it right!" Nuts squawked.

“I have to try—Speed Bump’s my best friend! Plus he’s TERRIBLE with directions! Even if he gets out of that purse, he’ll NEVER find his way back to the forest!”

Slingshot flew furiously away from the car, which was already starting to accelerate as it approached the highway on-ramp. Then he circled around and headed straight for the back window.

With his eyes closed and the wind pushing back the feathers on his face, Slingshot flew into the window opening at full speed.

He looked around and saw the wiggling purse.

I did it! he thought.

Then he realized that only half of him was actually in the car. His bottom half was still outside, his tail feathers flapping like a flag in a stiff wind. He was stuck, his belly wedged against the top of the window.

Nuts rolled his eyes and muttered, "What have I gotten myself into?" Then, with a burst of energy, the Nuthatch flew as fast as he could directly into Slingshot's bulging backside.

With a loud squawk, the two birds tumbled onto the cushioned seat. They smoothed their feathers and looked around. Music was blaring from the radio; the lady hadn't seen or heard their sudden appearance.

Hang on, *mon ami*! We're getting you out of there!
SLINGSHOT! You FOUND me!
Unzip this thing. It's dark and full of weird junk!

Slingshot grabbed the zipper with his beak and pulled while Nuts held on to the strap. The purse slowly opened. Speed Bump's head popped out like he was hatching from an egg all over again.

At that very moment, the car came to a stop.

"Houses! It's a neighborhood!" Nuts whispered. "She's home! HIDE!"

The three of them dove into a pile of old food wrappers under the front seat.

The back door of the car opened, and the lady reached in to grab her purse.

"GO!" Nuts hollered.

Wrappers went flying as the three birds shot out from under the seat. The lady screamed and dropped her purse. Slingshot snatched some food as he exited the car. None of them looked back as they rose into the blue.

French fry, anyone?
Uh, no.
Ew.

SIX

CHAPTER THAT DOESN'T RHYME WITH ANYTHING

"**W**ell, that was . . . um . . . interesting," Speed Bump said as he landed on the wire where Slingshot and Nuts were waiting.

Where have YOU been? Is that lotion on your head?
Hey, Nuts, your new friends are strange.
No offense.

Put an acorn in it, Jaybirds! That was an ADVENTURE! We had a blast, didn't we, guys? Didn't we? I sure did! Let's do it again sometime!

"Yeah. Sure. Maybe." Speed Bump yawned. "Right now, though, I just want to go home and take a nap."

"Me too," Slingshot agreed, yawning himself. Then a pained look came over his face.

"Au contraire, mon ami!" Speed Bump said, using the only French words he had learned from Slingshot. "C'mon, follow me."

And our last Bird Scout team is finally here! We thought you boys forgot about the meeting today. Did you complete the scavenger hunt?
practice sticks
B

Do you have something that turns, something that's pink, something that burns, and something that stinks?
Share your SEEDS!
No.

A huge smile appeared on Speed Bump's beak as he opened his overstuffed fanny pack.

Something that's PINK!
?
B
LW

Something that BURNS!
RED-HOT CINNAMON MINTS

AAAAANND...
Something that STINKS!
Parfum

You've earned new badges and hats, boys! CONGRATULATIONS!
I hereby declare Speed Bump and Slingshot official members of the EAGLE SCOUTS!

SEVEN

SERIOUSLY, WE'RE OUT OF RHYMES

Back at Speed Bump's home, the buddies were swooping and screeching in celebration when Slingshot suddenly stopped and got a puzzled look on his face.

"Wait a minute. We were together almost the whole time at the mall! Where did you get all that stuff for the scavenger hunt?"

Speed Bump stopped and turned to his friend. Slingshot paused, then his eyes lit up.

"THE PURSE!"

they said together, laughing.

I also got this.
A piece of green paper with an old man's face on it?
Weird, right?
Why would anyone ever collect **THIS**?
I don't know.
E
E
E

"Well, enough about treasures! I say we reward ourselves with some eagle food!" Slingshot declared. He flew out of the tree, and Speed Bump followed, doing his best to keep up.

Sounds great!
Er, as long as eagles don't eat worms.
Or cinnamon pretzels.
Urp

Slingshot looked over his wing and smiled.

Speed Bump sniffed the perfume trail as he followed his friend.

"Okay," he yelled. "But I don't think I'll have a problem finding you!"

Then the two of them swooped back down into the forest. Whatever happened next, they would be in it together.

QUESTIONS FOR THE AUTHOR

DAVE COVERLY

Were you a boy scout growing up? What sparked your imagination for *Night of the Living Shadows*?

I was actually a Cub Scout but never graduated to the Boy Scouts! Learning how to tie knots was just too difficult for my little bird brain, and don't even get me started on trying to make a birch-bark canoe.

However, as a Cub Scout I did enter the Pinewood Derby, where scouts have to carve a small car out of wood, add little wheels to it, and race other Cub Scouts' cars on a downhill track. My grandpa was a wood carver and all-around handyman, so he helped with the aerodynamics and showed me how to put metal weights inside the car to make it go fast. I painted my car red to make it look even faster, and on race day I fully anticipated coming home with the trophy.

And then I came in last. That may have been the beginning of the end of my Cub Scout days.

BUT: my favorite activity in the Scouts was definitely the Scavenger Hunt. There's something so satisfying about finding the specific thing you're looking for—sometimes I think maybe I should have been an archaeologist—and I still tend to collect stuff (music, magnets, books, dust . . .), so I thought maybe Speed Bump and Slingshot would have fun collecting their own little trinkets, too. Of course, when THEY collect stuff, it only leads them into another misadventure. . . .

What scenes were your favorite to write? To illustrate?
Writing a book is so fun once you get the "Big Idea" for what it's going to be about, because then you have to come up with smaller ideas that move the plot along. The smaller ideas are kind of like the rocks you step on to get across a stream. Once I had the idea that the buddies would go on a scavenger hunt to become Eagle Scouts and then end up in the mall, I had to

figure out how they would get out of the mall AND how they would still complete their task.

So my favorite part to write was near the end, when it turns out Speed Bump has actually found everything they need in the lady's purse where he was trapped. Not only did I think it was a fun surprise, but it also made sense, because birds are natural collectors. After all, that's how they make nests!

My favorite parts to draw were the scenes when they first get to the mall. In fact, I could hardly wait to get to the page where they're bouncing around on the massage chair! I really enjoyed having the birds interact with humans and human things, because it would all be so foreign to them. Being out of their natural element is what made the daytime scenes so fun, but that's what also made the nighttime scenes so nerve-wracking for them as well.

Can you tell us a little about what to expect in *Night of the Living Zombie Bugs*? (No spoilers, please!)
First, I can tell you that this misadventure is the creepiest of them all! Speed Bump and Slingshot hear rumors that there are large zombie bugs in the forest. With the help of some friends—and a strange old rook's map—they set out to prove that zombies are just a myth. But they're in for more than one surprise when they reach the far side of the forest. . . .

I hope you like it—and maybe some of you will even figure out the surprise before these bird buddies do!

What did you want to be when you grew up?
I knew in third grade that I wanted to be a cartoonist! Maybe because I loved to draw and use my imagination, and because being an adult seemed so weirdly complicated.

What's your most embarrassing childhood memory?

Oh, great, now I have to relive this. . . . When I was in seventh grade, I was the lead in a school play, and halfway through the most important scene, I totally forgot my lines. And it was the night the whole school and the parents were watching.

What's your favorite childhood memory?

When I was in sixth grade, my dog, Tigger, got off his leash and ran away. I thought he was just chasing a squirrel or exploring, but he didn't come back that day. Or the next day. Or the next! I remember being in school and being so sad that I couldn't even concentrate. On the fourth day that he was gone, I got off the bus to walk home, and as I came around the corner, I saw him in our garage, barking at me as I ran toward him. That has to be one of my happiest memories.

As a young person, who did you look up to most?

Definitely my parents. They didn't *tell* me how to act, they showed me, and they were wise enough to make sure I was paying attention. Even now, when a complicated situation comes up, I ask myself: What would my parents do? And if I'm still confused, I just call them. Because they're still around and they have a phone.

What was your favorite thing about school?

Doodling in the margins of my notebook.

Did you play sports as a kid?

I tried all kinds of sports! First baseball and football, and a little bit of soccer, but then I discovered tennis and fell in love with it. I played all the way through high school, and even got a scholarship to play in college. It's a great sport, because you can play it your entire life.

Where do you write your books?

I write my books in two different places, depending on what time it is. If it's late at night, I love to write in my studio, because it's in the attic of my house and it's very quiet and private. But if I write during the day, I LOVE to go outside and write on my porch. I live in a neighborhood where the houses are very old and close together, so while I'm writing I get to see the world going by and still feel like I'm a part of it.

What challenges do you face in the writing process, and how do you overcome them?

Writing can be very frustrating—you probably already know that! For me, it's very important that I have peace and quiet so I can get lost in the world of the characters. But since I work at home, sometimes I get interrupted by my dog barking, or by one of my kids asking me a question. Or I'll just get distracted because I'm hungry and the kitchen is right downstairs. So I set goals for myself about how much I have to do before I allow myself to take breaks.

What is your favorite word?

Foible. It sounds funny, and it also describes cartoons perfectly.

If you could live in any fictional world, what would it be?

Wait—this world isn't fictional?

Who is your favorite fictional character?

I love Gollum from *The Lord of the Rings*. He's so complicated—

sometimes you love him and sometimes you don't like him at all.

What was your favorite book when you were a kid? Do you have a favorite book now?

I have so many favorite books now! When I was really young, I read *The King, the Mice and the Cheese* over and over. When I got just a little bit older, I read all The Hardy Boys books and Encyclopedia Brown. I really liked mysteries—and I think Speed Bump and Slingshot might find themselves in a mystery of their own soon. . . .

What advice do you wish someone had given you when you were younger?

BUY STOCK IN APPLE COMPUTERS.

What would you do if you ever stopped writing?

Sleep.

If you were a superhero, what would your superpower be?

Flying. Like a bird. And then, like a bird, I might go to the bathroom on top of the houses of people I don't like. That's a superpower, right?

Do you have any strange or funny habits? Did you when you were a kid?

Okay, here's a crazy one that hardly anyone knows about me: Ever since seventh grade, I've always put my right shoe on first. ALWAYS. I'm not kidding. It would drive me crazy now to put my left shoe on first. I started it on a whim, and now it's forty years later and I'm still doing it. I don't even know why.

What would your readers be most surprised to learn about you?
I can shoot lasers out of my eyes. I just choose not to.

Disclaimer: No actual animals were hurt in the making of this book.

SQUARE FISH

After recovering from their terrifying escapades in the mall, Speed Bump and Slingshot investigate a potential zombie outbreak in their neck of the woods—but can these chickenhearted birds keep their cool?

KEEP READING FOR AN EXCERPT.

EARLY BIRD!

CHAPTER ZERO

THE BEGINNING OF THE END!

EARLY BIRD! EARLY BIRD! I NEED YOUR HELP!

Whoa, slow down, buddy! Want half of a worm?
This is no time for EATING! Not even for ME!

"It's Speed Bump! I can't wake him up! None of my usual tricks worked, not even taking off his headphones and yelling at him!"

"Did you try tipping over his nest?"

"Yes!" Slingshot cried. "I tried EVERYTHING!

"Oh, I hope he's not..." Slingshot couldn't even bring himself to finish that thought, it was so horrible.

"That DOES sound serious. Quick, Slingshot, follow me to my brother's hole in the tree!"

The pair flew through the forest as fast as their wings would take them.

Inside Speed Bump's room was a terrifying scene.

Slingshot shrieked.
Cheesable mercy, he's not just DEAD! He's a ZOMBIE!